Weekly Reader Children's Book Club presents

Mishmash

and the Venus Flytrap

By MOLLY CONE

Illustrated by Leonard Shortall

HOUGHTON MIFFLIN COMPANY BOSTON 1976

This book is a presentation of
The Popcorn Bag
Weekly Reader Book Club Senior Division

Weekly Reader Book Division offers book clubs for
children from preschool to young adulthood. All
quality hardcover books are selected by a distinguished
Weekly Reader Selection Board.

For further information write to:
Weekly Reader Book Division
1250 Fairwood Avenue
Columbus, Ohio 43216

Library of Congress Cataloging in Publication Data

Cone, Molly.
  Mishmash and the Venus flytrap.

  SUMMARY: As the owner of a Venus flytrap, Miss Patch
becomes suspicious when her dog Mishmash disappears.
  [1. Pets—Fiction. 2. Dogs—Fiction] I. Shortall,
Leonard W. II. Title.
PZ7.C7592Mkm   [Fic]   75-44380
ISBN 0-395-24376-9

Weekly Reader Children's Book Club Edition

To Ellen's Mindy
and also to Josh, Sami and Ilana

1

WANDA SPARLING was coming around the side of her house dragging an empty carton behind her. Wanda Sparling lived in the house next door to Pete Peters. If anyone had asked Pete whom he most easily could get along without, he would have had to say Wanda Sparling. She wasn't exactly one of his favorite classmates.

"Don't touch anything," she snapped as Pete followed Wanda and her box across the yard to her front porch.

Pete looked around. All he saw was a flowerpot sitting on the bottom step. A whiskery looking plant was growing in it.

"I'm not touching anything," he said, and stepped over it.

Wanda shrieked.

Pete turned so fast he almost knocked himself off the steps. "What's the matter with you?" he hollered at her.

"You almost did. That's what's the matter with me!" she said. "Although why I should worry my head over who you touch, I don't know."

"What do you mean—who?"

"I mean the plant, that's who," said Wanda.

Pete grinned. "A plant's not a who. It's an it," he told her.

"Not this plant," said Wanda positively. "My uncle sent that to me from Wilmington, South Carolina." She pulled the box around in front of it. "It's a very unusual plant. It's practically human."

Pete snorted. "No plant is human. They're not like people—or dogs," he added scornfully.

"Some are," said Wanda. "Some are just as human as dogs."

Pete laughed.

Wanda looked at him sharply. "Fact is, I'm thinking of giving this one to Miss Patch. For a pet."

Pete nearly fell off the porch laughing. His stomach began to hurt, he laughed so much.

Miss Patch was their teacher. Pete didn't bother to remind Wanda that Miss Patch already had a pet. She had Mishmash. Mishmash was the friendliest dog in the neighborhood. He was so friendly that everybody locked their doors to keep Mishmash from walking in.

Pete had given the big black dog to Miss Patch. Mishmash was the best present she had ever had. Miss Patch had said so. Mishmash was never too friendly for Miss Patch. She just laughed when Mishmash went to sleep in the middle of the bed with his head on the pillow. Or tried to sit on a chair, or rang the doorbell. She said that Mishmash was a very unusual dog.

Next to Mishmash, there wasn't anyone Pete liked better than Miss Patch. She opened her mouth and sang right out in school whenever she felt like it. When she talked, her teeth stuck out in a friendly smile. She was a very unusual teacher.

"She's exactly the kind of teacher who'd be crazy about this plant," said Wanda. "It catches flies."

"Mishmash catches flies," said Pete. "Any old fly that happens by. WAP! SMACK! That fly's got to look out for old Mishmash."

Wanda looked at him pityingly. "This plant not only catches flies, it also eats them."

Pete was still laughing. "What does Miss Patch need a plant that eats flies for?"

"I figure it would be sort of nice for Miss Patch to have a pet that gets its own food," said Wanda. "I figure it'd be nice for her not to have to worry about it digging holes in her yard. Or chewing up the

2

neighbors' geraniums. Or leaving anything behind that company will step into."

Pete stopped laughing.

Wanda went on talking. "It'd be a nice change, is what I'm thinking, for Miss Patch to have a pet that doesn't get hair on anyone's lap. Or open and close doors. Or thump in the middle of the night."

Pete scowled. "No old plant could take Mishmash's place, not with Miss Patch."

Wanda stood up. "Oh, I don't know. This won't be so much bother. It won't require a leash. Or a collar. Not even a flea collar. Because if a flea tried to bite it, it would be too bad for the flea."

Pete remembered how Mishmash kept Miss Patch up all night playing with an imaginary playmate. And how he kept the painter from finishing painting the house. And how he picked up souvenirs from the supermarket. And dumped things on the floor at the Laundromat. Pete remembered a lot of things suddenly.

Wanda picked up the potted plant and set it in the cardboard carton.

It was the same kind of box Wanda had helped him put Mishmash into as a present for the teacher. He remembered how Miss Patch had said, "Oh, my!" when she saw it sitting on the doorstep. He remembered how surprised she had been when she found Mishmash inside the carton. Pete could hear her voice lifting with excitement— "A present! For me?"

Pete stood there and watched Wanda put down the top flap and stick a card in an envelope. It was a fancy card with flowery letters on it that she had made herself. It said, "A Gift For You." He watched her lick the envelope and write the teacher's name on it. He watched her tape it to the top of a box.

"You can come along and help me carry it, if you want to," Wanda offered.

Pete made a noise that was supposed to be a laugh of scorn, but it

came out a squawk. "I'm not carrying that thing anywhere," he said.

"On second thought," said Wanda, "you'd do me a real favor if you didn't come. After all, I wouldn't want Miss Patch to think that this present came from both of us. If you get what I mean." She hoisted the box in her arms.

Pete watched her march down the walk, hating her. He hated her more than cobwebs in his face, or the color of blood, or eating stewed rhubarb and mashed green peas.

"A plant's not like a dog!" he hollered after her. He was sure of that anyway. As sure of that as he was of anything. "A plant can't do anything much!"

Wanda turned about slowly, pausing in the middle of the sidewalk. She leaned the box against her stomach. There was a smug expression on her face.

"That's true," she said sweetly. "That's perfectly true. One thing you can depend on this plant not doing—and that's BARK. You can absolutely depend on it."

2

PETE STOOD in front of his house looking after Wanda. He watched her go up the block. He watched her go past Mrs. Barnes' house and the Engstroms'. He watched her pass the Evans' and the Dooleys' and reach the corner. When she was definitely out of sight, he trailed after her. He moved up the street slowly as if he weren't going anywhere special. He stopped to peer at Mrs. Barnes' petunia borders and at the baby sleeping in a carriage in front of Mrs. Engstrom's house.

Mrs. Dooley looked over at him only a little suspiciously as he went by. Mrs. Dooley kept her bathroom door locked ever since Mishmash had looked in on her one day. Pete walked a little faster.

Mrs. Berty was just getting out of her little red car when he reached the corner. An old rocking chair was sticking out of the back end. Pete helped her lift the chair out and carry it up to her front porch.

"You didn't bring that big black dog along with you today, did you?" asked Mrs. Berty. She glanced a little nervously over her shoulder.

Pete shook his head.

But she looked back sharply at her car as if she expected to catch Mishmash sitting in the driver's seat.

Pete thought of Mishmash. Anyone could see that Mrs. Berty and Mishmash weren't exactly made for each other. You didn't even have to know that her doormat didn't say welcome on it, or that her

6

doorbell always buzzed flatly instead of making a nice loud ring.

"You'd better keep him off this chair," Mrs. Berty warned. "It's for my mother."

Pete looked at the chair's high back and skinny arms and crooked rockers.

"I got it at a garage sale," said Mrs. Berty. "It was a real bargain."

She sat down in it, placed her feet flat on the floor, and leaned forward to give the chair a good start. It creaked as it rocked back and forth. The screaking noise made Pete wince.

The sound pleased Mrs. Berty. She listened to it with her head to one side and a smile of satisfaction on her face.

She didn't have to worry about Mishmash sitting in it, thought Pete. Mishmash wouldn't want to sit in it. Mishmash didn't much like squeaking, or scraping, or bumping, or even rattling. The only noise he liked was the kind he made himself.

"My mother can sit all day and enjoy herself," Mrs. Berty said in a louder voice. She wanted to make sure she'd be heard over the sounds of the rocker.

Pete looked from the rocking chair out to the street. There wasn't much to see from Mrs. Berty's front porch. Except to watch the garbage truck and the mail lady go by. This was a dead-end street. It was even quieter than the one Mishmash and the teacher lived on. He gazed out over the tops of the trees and saw the wooden steeple on the church next door to the teacher's house.

Pete walked quickly up Cherry Street and down Pine. He passed the post office, the shoe repair shop, the bakery and the gas station. He started to run. He cut across to the next street, and went by the box hedge in front of the church, and the lilac clump.

His heart began to thump as he unlatched the gate to Miss Patch's house. But it wasn't because he had been hurrying.

For the first time, he noticed how many holes there were in Miss Patch's lawn. And the little brown spots. A lot of little brown spots.

He had never thought about all the little brown spots in the teacher's front lawn before. He noticed the straggly row of flowers. Some freshly planted ones seemed to be growing upside down. Pete regarded them a moment before closing the gate behind him.

An old rug lay halfway down the porch steps. On the porch was Wanda's box. It looked as if Wanda had put the carton on the porch and left it there. That's what it looked like, Pete thought hopefully.

He hoped Miss Patch and Mishmash had gone off somewhere together. To Victoria, perhaps, on the boat. Or maybe even to Europe. Pete grinned at the thought. That would be a good joke on Wanda. Her plant would just sit there by itself in the box until they came home. And when they did, they'd find nothing there but some little old dried up whiskers. Pete stood there at the gate and laughed out loud.

The box moved. The top of the carton popped open. Mishmash's head appeared, grinning. The dog leaped out of the box. His feet tangled with the carton flaps and he turned around and bashed at the thing with his paw.

The dog came tearing down the steps toward him. He slipped on the rug and slid forward. He picked himself up, yipping and yapping. He ran around Pete joyfully, jumping up to take swipes at Pete's face with his wet tongue.

"Good old Mishmash," Pete said, rubbing the dog's head. "Good dog! *Good* dog."

Suddenly, Pete wondered what he had been worrying about. Nothing could ever take the place of Mishmash with Miss Patch. Not another dog, or a cat, or a bird or fish or turtle. Not even a gerbil, or a hamster, or a trained flea.

And especially not Wanda's plant.

3

___

Miss Patch came out on her front porch to greet him. She was a familiar sight in her loose fitting sweater and old skirt with its uneven hem. Her black-rimmed glasses had slipped down, as usual, on her nose. Her teeth stuck out in a big smile.

"Come see my present!" she called to Pete.

Mishmash whirled around. He raced up the steps toward her. Miss Patch didn't step back hastily the way other ladies usually did. She stood there, her feet planted in her flat shoes, fondly smiling at the dog. Mishmash came to a skidding stop before her and smiled back. The teacher patted his head a couple of times and she held the screen door open.

Pete dragged his feet up the steps. He stepped over the pieces of carton strewn all over the porch. He and Mishmash walked in.

Miss Patch pointed to the flowerpot sitting on the kitchen table. The same pot with the same whiskery plant he had seen on Wanda's porch.

"It's a plant!" she said.

She didn't seem to notice that the window boxes were filled with plants. That the window sills were overflowing with them. Or that you couldn't see the house next door for the vines trailing all over the dining room window.

Pete looked at Wanda's plant. It had flat hairy leaves. Each pair of leaves was hinged together like an open clam shell. It didn't look like

9

anything to get excited about.

Mishmash looked at it too. He came closer to see it better.

"Watch," said Miss Patch. She put out a finger and tickled the inside of one of the leaves. It moved.

Mishmash blinked.

"It always moves when you touch it," Miss Patch said, and she sounded pleased. "It's a very sensitive plant."

Mishmash rested his nose on the table. He seemed immensely interested in the plant.

"It does so much more than ordinary house plants that just sit in flowerpots and soak up water," Miss Patch said.

Mishmash gave a sniff.

"It eats insects," Miss Patch said. "It's a carnivorous plant called *Venus flytrap*."

Mishmash began walking around the table. He slid his chin along the tabletop. He kept his eyes on the plant.

"Go out and play, Mishmash," Miss Patch said.

Mishmash put his front paws up on the table and moved his snout closer.

"Mish. Out," said Miss Patch.

The dog stuck out his paw and poked at the plant.

It moved. And so did Mishmash. He hurriedly backed away.

Miss Patch laughed. "That'll get you a free manicure," she told him. "Now out!" she said and opened the kitchen door for him.

Mish backed out. He went out the door and around the house and sat on the front porch and barked.

Miss Patch winced at the sound.

Hastily, Pete went out the door, too. He ran around the house and sat down next to Mishmash on the front porch. He put his arms around the big black dog. Mishmash was pleased. He put his paws on Pete's shoulders and wiped his tongue over Pete's face. He knocked Pete backwards and stepped all over him trying to hug him back. Pete

10

had to laugh in spite of himself.

Mishmash stood back, his tongue hanging wetly out of his mouth, his eyes shining. Then he lifted up his head and barked again.

"Shhh!" said Pete, frowning. He grabbed Mishmash by the collar and dragged him across the yard to the cover of the hydrangea bush. Somehow, it didn't surprise Pete to find Wanda sitting there.

"You'd better make him stop barking all the time," she advised.

Pete tried to pay no attention to her.

"And you've got to make him stop bothering the plant. Or—" Wanda picked up a twig and thoughtfully began to chew at it.

Pete stood up. He didn't let go of the dog's collar. "Or what?" he bellowed.

Wanda turned her head. She spit some shreds out of her mouth. The spittle landed on the fence. She seemed to be watching it glisten there under the sun. Then she tossed the twig over the fence and shrugged her shoulders.

"Or else . . ." she said.

4

PETE STARED down at the cereal in his bowl. He squinted at the raisins drowning in the milk. The sound of his voice went up and down in his throat. He could hear himself talking back to Wanda in his head. A sound fell from his lips.

"Eh?" said his father, looking up from his newspaper.

"Nothing," muttered Pete. He drank his glass of orange juice in a gulp.

His mother put a plate of scrambled eggs on the table and sat down too. "Mrs. Berty is expecting a visit from her mother," she said.

His father refolded the newspaper and continued to hold it while he was eating.

"She had the old radio fixed," Mrs. Peters said, "and bought a new color TV. She bought two feather pillows and a whole slew of knitting patterns and crochet books."

Pete tried to listen but his mind wasn't on Mrs. Berty's mother.

"Mrs. Berty is afraid that things are going to be a little too hectic for her mother around here. You know, people running in and out. The telephone ringing. Probably her mother will want to nap every afternoon. I guess it's not going to be all milk and honey."

Mr. Peters put his newspaper down. "Sounds like a fine arrangement to me."

"She's almost eighty years old," Mrs. Peters said.

Mr. Peters gave a sharp whistle. "How is she getting here? She's not travelling alone, is she?"

Mrs. Peters hesitated. "Well, that's what Mrs. Berty doesn't quite know. She couldn't make any sense out of the postcard she received. It didn't tell what airline and what flight her mother was coming on. Mrs. Berty couldn't alert the stewardess to keep an eye on her."

"And?"

"Well, the postcard rambled. Her mother wrote something about exploring the countryside and meeting new companions. But she forgot to put in the vital information."

Mr. Peters chuckled. "You can't expect an old lady to be sharp as a tack."

Mrs. Peters sighed. "I guess Mrs. Berty will have her hands full."

Pete pushed his chair back. "Anyway, she's got a rocking chair," he said and walked out the back door.

When Pete reached the teacher's house, the sound of singing was rolling out the window. The window in the house next door slammed down. As Miss Patch said, she was no opera star.

Pete knocked. He listened to the singing awhile and knocked some more. Pretty soon the singing stopped. Miss Patch was talking to Wanda's plant and it seemed to be listening.

Pete rang the bell. Both Miss Patch and Mishmash came to the door together.

Miss Patch held open the screen door. "Come on in and say hello to my plant," she said, and she went into the bedroom.

Pete walked into the kitchen and stood there looking at the Venus flytrap. He couldn't imagine himself saying hello to a plant. Not to any plant. But particularly not to this plant.

"Venus likes to be talked to," Miss Patch called in from the other room. "It's amazing how fast a plant grows when you make a habit of saying something to it."

Pete leaned closer to the plant. He said something to it. He said— "Go jump in the river." But he didn't say it loud enough for Miss

14

Patch to hear—only the plant.

"Come on, Mishmash," he said then.

But Mishmash was busy chasing a fly. It must have gotten in when the screen door was held open.

"It's really a very interesting species," Miss Patch said. Her head was in the closet, but her voice, as always, was nice and loud. "I went to the library to look it up. Its natural home is a bog. You wouldn't believe how effective it is in catching its own food."

Mishmash jabbed his paw at the fly in the air. It buzzed up and away. He became smarter. He lay low, not twitching a muscle. His eyes moved with the movements of the fly. The dog watched the fly alight on the table. Then slowly Mishmash raised his head.

He watched the fly buzz up the side of the bowl. Stealthily his paw moved closer. He watched the fly alight on the edge of a leaf. The hairs on the leaf quivered. And Mishmash tensed to make a quick thrust. The fly stepped forward. Mishmash lunged. But so did the plant. A pair of leaves snapped shut. The fly was gone.

Mishmash stood up with his forepaws on the table and stared at the plant.

Pete heard a sharp buzzing sound from within the closed pod. And then silence.

Pete couldn't help himself. He shuddered.

"It works like a bear trap," Miss Patch said. She came into the kitchen and stood there looking proudly down at the plant. "The fly or ant is drawn to it because of a sweet smell. But it has tiny trigger hairs on the surfaces of the leaves. When anything brushes against them, the trap snaps shut."

Mishmash was sniffing at the floor. He stuck his nose up toward the ceiling, as if he expected to see the fly buzzing around.

"Fascinating, isn't it?" said Miss Patch happily. "No one knows how the Venus flytrap eats its victims. It's a real mystery. Even to scientists. All they've been able to figure out is that the Venus flytrap

15

takes about ten days to digest its victim. Then its pods open up again and it gets ready to trap something else."

Mishmash whined. He came to stand near Miss Patch. He leaned against her.

"Go out and play, Mishmash," Miss Patch said. She pushed him away.

He barked.

"Be quiet, Mishmash," the teacher said.

Mishmash sat back and barked again.

"Stop that, Mishmash," Miss Patch said crossly. "You're bothering my plant."

"Take him out, Pete," she said. "Take him for a walk, or something." She had already turned her back on the dog.

"Come on, Mishmash," said Pete. He dragged him out of the kitchen. He opened the screen door and pushed the big black dog out. But Mishmash wouldn't go for a walk. He just sat on the doormat and howled.

5

PETE DRAGGED Mishmash under the hydrangea bush and made him sit down. He held the dog's mouth closed with his hands.

Mishmash tried to shake off Pete's hands. He tried to bark. Little barks dribbled out of his closed snout.

"Quiet!" Pete ordered firmly. Still holding the dog's jaws gently but firmly together, he put his mouth close to one black ear. "You hear me? I said QUIET!"

The dog jumped. He rolled his eyes wide at Pete. He seemed surprised. He seemed so surprised that Pete felt like giving him a reassuring hug. But he held himself back.

"Now, what you've got to do from now on is stop barking. You understand?" Pete spoke slowly and very clearly. "STOP BARKING." Then he eased his hold on the dog's mouth.

"Whiff!" said Mishmash experimentally.

Pete clamped down on the dog's jaws again. He wrapped both hands around the snout. He gazed severely into the dog's dark eyes. "No," he said. And then he said it louder. "NO."

The dog's eyes gazed thoughtfully back at him. Suddenly he yanked away from Pete's grasp. But he didn't bark. He sat there solemnly, face to face with Pete.

Squatting before Mishmash, Pete gazed back, eyeball to eyeball.

The dog grinned.

Pete frowned.

Mishmash stopped grinning. He raised his head. "Whiff! Whiff!"

Quickly Pete fastened his hands around the dog's jaw again. Mishmash tried to back away. Pete's grip held. The dog whined.

Pete loosened his hold. He sat before the dog and he talked. Pete told Mishmash all the reasons why he had to stop barking. He enumerated them one by one. He gave many reasons—but he didn't give the dog the real one. Pete just couldn't bring himself to tell Mishmash that Miss Patch might replace him as a pet with Wanda's plant.

Mishmash listened. He didn't seem to mind listening. His eyes stayed on Pete's face. His head nodded every sentence or two as if he understood. Pete began to feel pretty good. He began to feel that he was really making his point. After all, Mishmash was not an ordinary dog. He was definitely smarter than most other dogs. He was even smarter than a lot of people. Pete talked on and on. He talked so much that his voice began to get hoarse.

Mishmash was attentive. He just sat there, hardly twitching, with his eyes wide open. Pete stopped talking. He gave Mishmash a loving pat on the head. The dog's eyes closed and opened again. Pete turned Mishmash around and set him in the direction of Miss Patch's front porch.

He patted the dog's rump. "Now, go, Mishmash," Pete said. "Go. And remember—be quiet!"

Pete stayed there under the hydrangea bush, kneeling on his hands and legs while he watched. Mishmash trotted across the lawn, up the steps, and onto the front porch. Pete watched as Mishmash plopped down in a shady spot and sat there, his eyes still wide open, regarding the flowers swaying in the breeze.

Not a woof came out of his mouth. Not a whiff, not a whine.

Pete crawled out from under the hydrangea bush and started home. He walked briskly, swinging his arms and his legs. He held his chest out. He couldn't help but feel pretty proud of himself. One thing he knew about was dogs, he told himself. He could depend on it for sure. Mishmash no longer would be bothering Wanda's plant by barking.

As he went up the street toward Mrs. Berty's house, Pete heard the sound of rocking. Squeeeeeek—squueel. Squeeeeeeeek—squueel. He listened as he walked. He could hear it plainly all the way up the block.

Pete guessed that Mrs. Berty's mother had arrived. Mrs. Berty was probably pleased that her mother was already sitting on her front porch, rocking in the rocking chair and enjoying the view of the street.

Pete looked curiously toward Mrs. Berty's porch as he went by. He saw the rocking chair briskly rocking. Pete stopped.

He saw the rocking chair going back and forth, back and forth. It was teetering wildly. The chair runners were hitting the floor boards in a bumpy rhythm. Squeeeeeek—squueel. Squeeeeeeeek—squueel.

Pete stood there and stared at the moving rocker. No one was sitting in it.

6

————————

"MRS. BERTY'S mother arrived from California," said Pete's mother.

His father helped himself to some more coffee. Pete started on his milk.

"She hitchhiked," his mother said.

Mr. Peters set down his coffee cup and missed the saucer.

"It was a very pleasurable trip she said," Mrs. Peters said.

"You mean that old lady travelled all the way up from California hitchhiking?" Pete's father said.

"She doesn't like riding in planes. And buses make her feet itch."

"But that's at least 900 miles!"

"She likes backpacking and camping out," Mrs. Peters said. "She carried her own sleeping bag. She said she met a lot of nice people hitchhiking."

Pete's father laughed. "Can't you just see that little old lady standing on the highway with her thumb stuck out?"

"It sounds sort of marvelous to me," Pete's mother said.

"Well it sounds crazy to me," said Pete's father. "Any eighty-year-old woman who runs around the country acting like a teenager must be absolutely dotty."

Pete thought about the rocking chair rocking all by itself on Mrs. Berty's porch. He looked out the window. He saw Wanda going past his house. She was walking as if she wore a crown on her head and a procession followed behind her. She was holding her hands out stiffly in front of her. In them she carried a platter. On the platter was what appeared to be a cake. A lopsided one.

"Excuse me," said Pete and he dashed out the back door. "You, Wanda!" he bawled at her. "Where do you think you're going?"

She turned around. "Visiting," she said in her company voice. "I'm going to officially welcome Mrs. Berty's mother to the neighborhood. You might say I'm the welcoming committee."

Pete walked along behind her.

"You might as well come along," she said without any enthusiasm. "Only don't pretend the cake is from both of us. I didn't slave over a hot stove all day just to make a present from you."

Pete had had quite enough of Wanda's presents. He pretended he wasn't really interested.

The rocking chair was there on Mrs. Berty's porch. It was rocking again, all by itself. Wanda almost dropped her cake.

Cautiously, they moved up the walkway. The front door was open. Suddenly, Mrs. Berty's voice came singing out.

"Mother?" she called. "You enjoying yourself?"

A voice came from behind the bushes screening part of the porch. "Oh yes," it said heartily. "Yes, indeedy."

A hand reached out and pushed at the empty chair. The chair began to rock faster. It creaked violently. Wanda gasped.

A little old lady stuck her head up. Her hair was grey, her face wrinkled.

"Hi," said Pete.

"Hi," she said, and came around to the top of the steps. She was wearing a yellow-striped T shirt. And blue jeans. There was a red bandanna sticking out of her back pocket.

Stiffly, Wanda walked up the steps. She laid the cake down on the porch. "My mother sent this cake," she said.

Pete nudged her. "You baked it."

"I baked it," she said.

"The welcoming committee," he prompted.

"It's made of prunes," she said.

"Sit down," said the old lady. She glanced at Wanda's party dress. Then she pulled out the red bandanna from her back pocket and laid it on the top step. Wanda sat down on it gingerly. She folded her hands in her lap and pressed her knees close together.

Mrs. Berty's mother sat down herself. But not on the rocking chair. She plopped down on the porch steps, too.

"I never had a welcoming committee before," she said. She bent her head and gazed at the lopsided cake. "I never ate my prunes in a cake before either." Without even turning her head, she reached out and gave the rocking chair another push.

Wanda stared at the creaking chair.

"You all right, Mother?" Mrs. Berty's voice sang out again from inside.

The old lady made a face. "Just fine!" she hollered. She stuck out her foot and gave the chair a bigger push. Obediently, it bumped and creaked again.

She jerked her head in the direction of the front door. "Makes her happy to think I'm sitting in it." She winked. Both eyes at the same time. "Most of the time I just start it going and sit where I want to."

Suddenly Wanda grinned. She let her shoulders slump back into their natural position. She pushed her sock down and scratched at her leg.

"I see what you mean," she said.

"My daughter treats me like an old lady." Mrs. Berty's mother grimaced. "That's the trouble with middle-agers. They think being old is the same as being sick. I don't know how many people have told me—'Berty, you can't do that.' But I do it anyway."

"Like hitchhiking," said Pete.

"I built my own house," she said. "With my own hands. Designed it myself, too. Did it all from books on carpentry and house building I got out of the library. You want to see something?"

She pulled at some stuff in her back pocket and brought out a card. She handed it to Pete.

He turned it over in his hands. It looked like a credit card.

"It's a carpenter's union card. Master carpenter. It's mine."

She put it back into her pocket again. "Of course, I got it a long time ago. Everybody said you can't. But I did."

She stuck her finger out and jabbed at the frosting on the cake. She placed her finger in her mouth.

"That's a good cake," she said to Wanda. "For prunes."

Mrs. Berty appeared in the doorway. "Oh my," she said. She didn't notice that the rocking chair was still rocking a little. "We have company. Isn't that nice."

Wanda stood up. "We just brought a little welcome cake," she said in her mother's voice. "It's for your dinner."

Mrs. Berty picked it up. "Well, isn't that nice." She turned to her mother. Raising her voice slightly, she said, "That's certainly thoughtful, isn't it, Mother?"

"Thoughtful," said her mother obediently.

Wanda jabbed her elbow at Pete. He rose hastily.

"You must come again soon for another little visit with Mother," Mrs. Berty said.

Pete followed Wanda down to the sidewalk. They heard the door bang behind Mrs. Berty. They heard the creak of the rocking chair again.

Wanda began to giggle. She stuffed her hands into her mouth to hold back the sound. It sounded as if she were drinking soup.

Pete looked away. Sometimes the sight of Wanda was more than he could stomach.

7

"MISHMASH is asleep," said Miss Patch when she opened the door to Pete. She stood there in her bathrobe, yawning.

"Asleep?" Mishmash never slept this late, thought Pete. "What's the matter with him?"

Miss Patch rubbed her eyes with her hands. "That's what I'd like to know," she said. Her teeth were sticking out, but not in a friendly smile.

Pete followed her into the living room. The sofa pillows were on the floor. The rug was askew. One of the window shades hung down off its roller, as if someone had taken a swipe at the window and missed.

"He was catching flies," she said. And she yawned again. "Or that's what I think he was trying to do. He spent the whole night chasing them." She picked up one of the sofa pillows. "He polished all the windows with his nose, trying to get close enough to grab one. He stood right up on the sofa," she said, "and batted at the ceiling."

She tossed the pillow back onto the sofa and didn't notice that it slipped right down to the floor.

"He ran around in circles, swatting at the air. He ran into the wall twice." She shuddered. "I thought the whole house was coming down."

Miss Patch scratched at her elbow. "Every few minutes he came tearing into my bedroom to wake me up. Can you imagine? Waking

me up out of a perfectly sound sleep just to make me watch him chasing flies?"

Pete shuffled his feet instead of answering.

"That went on all night," Miss Patch said. And her voice rose a little higher. "All night!" She shook her head hopelessly. "He never did this before. I can't understand it."

Pete went into the bedroom and stared at Mishmash. He was sound asleep on the couchbed in Miss Patch's room. His head was on a pillow. One paw was tucked in under his chin. He looked tired. Tired and peaceful. As if he had had a successful night.

Pete bent his head down to Mish's ear. "There's got to be some changes around here," he warned. "You hear me?"

The dog's nose twitched. One eyelid opened and shut. Then a loud snore came rolling out between his lips. Or was it a snort? Pete stared at the dog. He wasn't sure.

"Sleeping like a baby," said Miss Patch. But there was no fondness in her voice. She sat down on her own bed. She yawned again. "Be sure to lock the back door on your way out," she said.

Pete went into the kitchen. He looked at the Venus flytrap plant sitting on the table. He wondered what Mishmash had been trying to do all night.

He watched an ant crawl over the sphagnum moss. It stopped to rub two legs together and proceeded onward. He watched it bob up and down the hills of dirt. It crawled onto a leaf pod and moved toward the open trap.

He watched it get nearer and nearer the waiting trap. He could see, almost feel, the plant hairs quiver, waiting for the ant to touch them. The plant moved. And so did Pete. He stuck his finger in front of the ant and knocked it off. Then he picked the ant up on a pinch of soil and carried it out the back door. He dropped it safely onto the earth below the window.

8

"MY MOTHER is having a party," Wanda told him. "For Mrs. Berty's mother. She spent the morning down at the beauty parlor having her hair fixed. She met Mrs. Berty down there having her hair fixed, too."

"I bet Mrs. Berty's mother isn't having her hair fixed for anybody's party," said Pete.

"She doesn't have to," said Wanda. "Mrs. Berty bought her mother a wig. It's the latest style wig. 'It's going to make her mother look ten years younger,' my mother said."

"What does she want to look ten years younger for?"

"My mother said all old people like to look younger."

"Only if they don't like being old."

"Well, who likes being old?" Wanda patted her own hair and shook out the full long skirt she was wearing.

"Mrs. Berty's mother doesn't mind," said Pete. "She doesn't care how old she is. If she were a hundred and eleven years old it wouldn't bother her any."

"Well it bothers Mrs. Berty," said Wanda. "It bothers her so much that she's not sitting out in the sun anymore."

"She's going to grow just as old sitting in her living room as out in the sun," Pete pointed out.

"But she won't have as many wrinkles. The sun gives you wrinkles," said Wanda.

"What's wrong with wrinkles?" asked Pete.

"Wrinkles make you *look* old." Wanda got up, smoothed her skirt again, and opened the screen door.

"Mrs. Dale's baby is all wrinkled and it's not old," Pete hollered at her. "It's new. Brand new."

Wanda let the screen door bang behind her.

*

"Mrs. Sparling is having a party," his mother said when he came stamping into the house.

Pete glared at her.

"She said Wanda particularly wanted you to come, too."

"I'm not going," said Pete.

His mother was taking things out of one purse and putting them into another. "You'd better change your shirt, if you're going," she said.

"I'm not going."

His mother brushed at her skirt. "You might as well wash your face, too. It's not clean enough for a party."

"I'm not going."

His father came down the stairs with his fishing tackle box. "Where are you not going to?" he inquired.

"To Mrs. Sparling's party," Pete said.

"Sounds like a very good idea," said Mr. Peters as he went into the kitchen with his fishing stuff.

Pete's mother sighed and went off to the party without him.

Pete went out the door and sat on the front porch. He stayed there awhile watching everybody in the neighborhood come to Mrs. Sparling's party.

When Mrs. Barnes arrived, she glanced over at him and peered around uneasily. "You haven't got that big black dog with you today,

29

have you?'' Mrs. Barnes anxiously asked.

Regretfully, Pete shook his head. He wished he did have Mishmash here with him. Mishmash loved parties. Pete watched Mrs. Barnes go up the steps to Mrs. Sparling's house. She stood there ringing the doorbell even though the door was wide open. Once his mother had had a party and Mishmash had pushed Mrs. Barnes into the coat closet and closed the door. Pete sat there grinning.

Wanda came out on the porch carrying some folding chairs. She tripped over her long skirt and fell flat on the floor.

"What are you laughing at?'' she yelled over at him.

"I'm not laughing at you," Pete said. "I'm laughing at Mishmash."

She leaned over the porch railing. "He's not invited to this party," she warned. "My mother says she's got enough to worry about without having Mishmash around. She says if she sees him here today, she's going to take my father's BB gun and give him you-know-what you-know-where. That's what she says."

"It's against the law to shoot out of season. My father said so," said Pete.

"The law," said Wanda, "is for hunters. They're not supposed to kill animals."

"Well, Mishmash is an animal. He's a dog, isn't he?"

Wanda stuck her face out toward him. "You bet he is," she said. "And he'd better not forget it!"

Mrs. Berty's red car stopped in front of the house. Mrs. Berty got out, and then Mrs. Berty's mother. That is, Pete guessed it was Mrs. Berty's mother. Though he wasn't exactly sure.

She wore a bright pink dress and shiny new shoes. Her hair looked new too. It was piled up on top of her head in the latest style. It looked a little like Wanda's prune cake.

Mrs. Berty grabbed hold of her mother's arm. "Now careful, Mother," she said. "Mind the walk. It's a little uneven."

Mrs. Berty's mother shook off her daughter's hand. "I've been walking by myself all my life," she said. She went charging on ahead.

For the first part of the party, the ladies stood on the porch shrieking compliments at each other.

"Your hair!" Pete heard Mrs. Barnes saying to Mrs. Berty's mother. "How beautiful it is! How ever do you keep it looking so nice?"

A plain voice rose out of the babble. "I just take it off," Mrs. Berty's mother said, "and put it in my top drawer."

Pete rushed into his house and stuck his head into the closet to laugh.

"Well, how was the party?" Pete's father said later.

Pete's mother sighed.

"What's the matter?" said his father. "Didn't it come off?"

"Oh, it was a lovely party," Mrs. Peters said. "A perfectly lovely party." But she didn't sound as if she meant it.

"Anybody drink tea out of a saucer?" inquired Pete's father. "Anybody forget to say thank you for the cake? Anybody drop their teeth in the teapot?"

Pete's mother shook her head. "Poor Mrs. Berty," she said. "She's at her wits' end."

Mr. Peters began to look interested.

"Her mother showed everybody her carpenter's union card."

Mr. Peters slapped his knees and chortled. "Well, I'd like to have seen that!"

"She said she'd like to do a little fishing while she's here."

"Good for her!" Pete's father said, still laughing. "You just tell her she might go out to the end of the old dock and drop a line down. She might just catch herself a minnow."

"She plans to catch herself a salmon," said Pete's mother.

Pete's father stopped laughing. "She WHAT?"

"Salmon," said Pete's mother. "A King salmon."

31

Pete's father took a step or two in one direction, then a step or two in the other. "You can't just go out and catch a salmon," he spluttered. "It's not like digging potatoes out of the garden. You've got to know how to cut herring for bait. You've got to know about sinkers and reels and lures and flashers and line. You just tell her that!" he said.

Mrs. Peters smiled. "Mrs. Berty said she doesn't know how many times she's said—'Mother, you can't do that.' But her mother goes ahead and does it anyway."

"Beats me why that woman doesn't have sense enough to act her age," Pete's father said shaking his head. And he kept shaking his head, talking and muttering to himself.

"Speaking of age," said Pete's mother. "I think the upstairs bathroom could use a coat of paint."

Mr. Peters looked vaguely up at the ceiling.

"The bathroom?" he said.

"Upstairs," Pete's mother said.

"I don't have to go to the bathroom," his father said.

Pete giggled.

"Oh, for heaven's sake!" said Mrs. Peters. "The bathroom. It needs painting."

Pete's father threw his hands in the air. He went upstairs and soon came down again.

"It looks just fine to me," he declared.

9

THE TEACHER'S front door was open. Pete could see her inside, sweeping. She had her hat on. She was shoving something into the dustpan. She was carrying it out the front door, and across the porch, and dumping it into the shrubbery.

"Hi, Miss Patch." Pete closed the gate behind him.

Mishmash came skidding around the corner of the house. His eyes shone like light bulbs. His tongue hung down red and wet.

Pete laughed at the sight. "Down, Mish." Pete patted and pushed the big head out of his face. "He sure is happy to see me," he said proudly to Miss Patch.

Mishmash sat back. He stretched his mouth wide. It looked like a big grin.

Miss Patch came down the steps. The same black-rimmed glasses sat on her nose. But somehow she looked different. And it wasn't just her hat. Maybe it was because her teeth weren't sticking out. And that was because she wasn't smiling. She leaned down and shook the dustpan in front of Mishmash's nose.

The grin went off the dog's face—promptly. But the glimmer stayed there in his eyes.

Miss Patch turned to Pete and waved the dustpan at him. "You know what he did?"

Pete held his nose. He didn't want to know what Mishmash had done. He knew already. But she told him anyway.

He watched the teacher go into the house and firmly close the door behind her. Then he frowned at Mishmash.

"Now look here, Mishmash. You've got to cut that out. You understand? Cut it out!"

Mishmash raised his head.

"No more hunting flies in the middle of the night."

Mishmash looked back into Pete's eyes. Pete cleared his throat. "And no more doing it on the living room rug. And that's final."

Mishmash opened his mouth ever so slightly and burped.

Then he turned around and walked away from Pete, past the shrubbery and around the corner of the house. Pete went home.

"How's Venus?" asked Wanda.

Pete glared at her. "I don't know," he said. "And I don't care. What's more, Mishmash doesn't care either."

Wanda shrugged. "Sibling rivalry," she said.

Pete stared at her blankly.

"Surely you know what sibling rivalry is?"

"Oh, surely," said Pete quickly. "I surely do. Who wouldn't?" He slapped his knee. "Ha Ha. Surely I do!"

Wanda said, "It's jealousy between sisters and brothers."

"Mishmash hasn't any sisters or brothers," Pete reminded her. "He was an orphan. He was brought up in a palace—well, at least it was a place as big as . . ."

Wanda sniffed. "Mishmash is jealous of Venus. Just as jealous as if they were brother and sister. The first child is always jealous when the second child in the family arrives. It's a known fact."

She patted her hair. "You should have seen how my sister acted when I was born. She had tantrums. She wet her pants. She stole my bottle and drank it. She wanted all my mother's attention for herself. She—" Wanda paused and looked at him pityingly. "It's something you wouldn't understand—you being an *only* child."

Pete laughed. He rolled on the ground laughing. He made so

much noise that Wanda's mother stuck her head out the upstairs window to see what was going on.

"WANDA!" Her voice shot out over the top of the rose bushes. It fell squarely on their heads. "I'm going to spank the living daylights out of you if you don't stop beating up on your playmates!"

Pete stopped laughing.

The window slammed down.

Wanda smiled. "My mother is against violence. She says there is so much violence being shown on TV these days, that kids are growing up knowing nothing but mayhem and murder. She says what she's going to do is start an anti-violence campaign right here in this neighborhood. Right now she's pretty busy monitoring all the TV shows. She's making a list . . ."

Pete got up and walked away.

Wanda yelled after him. "Not everybody is always so nice and sweet and gentle and kind and *perfect* as you," she hollered. "It's a violent world! And you'd better just believe it!"

10

MISS PATCH looked distraught. Her hair had a crooked part and her sweater was on backward.

"You know what Mishmash is doing?" she said as soon as she opened the door to Pete.

Pete looked past her toward the kitchen. Mishmash lolled in the kitchen doorway. His big body filled it completely. He grinned when he saw Pete. He grinned and thumped his tail against the floor.

"He's not doing anything," said Pete. "He's just sitting there."

"He's not just sitting there!" said Miss Patch.

Pete shook his head. He couldn't see that Mishmash was doing anything else. He wasn't even barking.

"He won't go in and he won't come out," the teacher said.

Mishmash yawned.

"He isn't letting one insect, not one single, solitary fly, ant, or spider get near that plant!"

"You don't say," said Pete, and for some reason he felt a little guilty.

"He's starving the plant!" said Miss Patch.

"I see what you mean," said Pete, and he tried not to smile.

"That's his strategy. I know it." She sounded a little hysterical.

Pete looked severely at the big black dog. "Get out of there, Mishmash," he said. But his voice didn't carry much force.

Miss Patch folded her arms around her chest and glared at the dog.

"There are going to be some changes around here," she warned.

Pete took hold of the dog's collar. Mishmash didn't resist, not noticeably, that is. He just slumped down, perfectly relaxed.

"Come on, Mish," said Pete. "We're going out for a walk." He pulled at the dog.

It was like getting a huge blob of tar off the street. Pete finally dragged him, still plopped down, across the bare floor and out the door.

Once outside, Mishmash stood up. He stretched out each of his legs, one after the other, and ran around the house.

Pete followed him around. Mishmash was up on the back porch again, rattling the doorknob.

"MISH!" Pete hollered.

The dog paid no attention to him.

"You come here, Mishmash! You hear me? Come here."

Mishmash stood up on his hind legs and pressed his nose against the window.

Pete went up there. He grasped the dog's collar and dragged him off the porch. Mishmash put his backside down. He allowed himself to be pulled around to the front of the house, out the front gate. Then he got up on all four legs.

Pete kept his hand on the dog's collar. He kept pulling him along up the street.

"Now look here, Mish," Pete scolded. "There's one thing you've got to do, and that is stop messing around with that plant. You got me?" They passed the church.

"You've got to live and let live," he said as they left the gas station behind. "You're not the only fish in the sea. You're not the only pebble on the beach. You're not the only leaf on the tree."

Mishmash trotted along beside Pete. He seemed willing enough to go now. Pete eased his hold on the dog's collar.

"What you've got to learn," Pete said more kindly, "is to share."

Mishmash speeded up a little.

"Sharing is very important," Pete went on a little more loudly as the dog began pulling him forward.

They went past Mrs. Berty's house. The rocker was on the porch but it wasn't rocking. Mrs. Berty's mother was coming around the side of the house. She was wearing her jeans and red bandanna. She had a tool box in her hand.

"Hi," Pete called. But the old lady didn't hear him. And Mishmash didn't wait for Pete to say hello again. He just yanked him along.

"All right," Pete said to the dog. "All right. All right. So we'll go to my house. Just for a little while. You understand? I'll let you stay in my room for a while. Maybe just until after dinner." He grabbed hold of the dog's collar more firmly again.

"But you've got to behave yourself. You got that? No taking a bath with my mother's bath soap. No snitching my father's newspaper. No pushing people into closets. Or switching the channels on the TV."

The dog dragged Pete up his front walk and around to the back door. His tail pounded on the porch boards as Pete looked into the kitchen. No one seemed to be about.

"Quiet!" warned Pete.

The tail stopped thumping.

The dog stayed close to Pete as they crossed the kitchen. They sneaked into the hallway and scrambled up the stairs. Pete heard his mother coming up from the laundry room in the basement. He heard her start up the stairs.

"Psssst!" He motioned to Mishmash. And he noiselessly opened his bedroom door.

A woman stood in the middle of his room. "SURPRISE!" she said.

Pete's hand froze on the doorknob. He saw her sweater on his bed,

her suitcase open on his chair. A bracelet jangled on her wrist.

"Remember me?" she said. "I'm your Aunt Edith."

She advanced toward him. She grabbed his shoulders. She put a hand on each side of his face. And she held on to his head tightly while she plastered a kiss on his forehead.

Mishmash backed away. He turned around and bolted. He disappeared down the stairs before Pete could breathe again. Pete saw him through the window, running. He was heading back toward Miss Patch's house.

"I knew you'd be surprised to see me," said his Aunt Edith.

His mother came into the bedroom carrying colored sheets.

"Aunt Edith will sleep in your room," she said. "I've moved your things downstairs. You can sleep on the living room sofa tonight." She sounded a little nervous.

Pete's Aunt Edith always made his mother nervous. She never let them know when she was coming. The minute she arrived, she began to make suggestions on how to improve everything about the place.

"Hi," said Pete politely, and he started out of the room.

His Aunt Edith turned around. Pete could feel her eyes on the back of his head.

"He needs vitamins," Aunt Edith pronounced before Pete had reached the end of the hallway.

*

"You make me sick," Pete said to Wanda. He flopped down on her front steps and glared at her.

"So what else is new?" she said.

"You know what I'm talking about."

"Sure I do. Mishmash. Who else. You'd think that animal was the only dog in the neighborhood. You'd think he was the only dog in the city of Tacoma. The only one in the state of Washington. You act as

41

if he were the only dog in the whole United States of America. *Including* Hawaii and Alaska. Maybe even the only one on this planet Earth. That's what you think.''

''He's gone to war with your plant,'' said Pete.

Wanda sat back. She pursed her lips. She stared up at the sky.

''Did you hear me? I said he's out for blood. You know what that means?''

Wanda's head turned toward him. Her eyes squinted in the bright sunlight. ''I wonder who'll win,'' she said.

11

PETE'S AUNT EDITH had been visiting them only two days and she had already moved the living room furniture around. Pete closed the door. He walked around the table that had been sitting in the upstairs hallway and was now pushed against the stairway wall. He stopped to look at the pictures on the wall.

"Why don't you paint the woodwork in this room cream?" he heard his Aunt Edith say. Her voice was hoarse. Probably from talking so much, thought Pete.

She had a scarf stuck around her head, and she wore peach-colored cotton pants. The kind that are supposed to look wrinkled and certainly do. She looked a little like Pete's father. But not much.

His mother's face had a pinched look, as if she had been downtown shopping all day and her feet hurt.

"Why don't you add a little diced Italian salami to the eggs next time you scramble them," Aunt Edith suggested at lunchtime.

"I like them this way," Pete's father said.

"Which reminds me," said Aunt Edith. "Have you taken this boy shopping lately? He needs new jeans. The ones he's wearing are practically in shreds."

"I like them this way," Pete said.

"Why don't you jog around the block every morning?" his Aunt Edith advised his father when she saw him with his sweater buttoned all the way down over his middle. "Jogging is so good for keeping the stomach flat," Aunt Edith said with conviction.

Pete's mother said, "I like him this way," but his Aunt Edith didn't even hear her.

Neither did Pete's father. "You really think so?" he said to his sister. And he got up and went to look at himself in the mirror.

"The bathroom could use a coat of paint," Aunt Edith said when she came down to dinner that evening.

"A very good idea," Pete's father said, as if it had never occurred to anybody.

When Pete woke up on the living room sofa the next morning, he couldn't figure out where he was for a moment. His father's chair had moved from one side of the fireplace to the other. The bedroom radio was in the bathroom. The living room clock was in the hallway. It was a relief to find his mother in the kitchen just as usual.

"What's for breakfast?" Pete asked, sitting down at the kitchen table.

"Cooked oatmeal," said his mother. Her voice sounded mushy.

"What are we having oatmeal for?" Pete asked. His mother didn't especially like oatmeal. He didn't like it much himself unless it was filled with raisins and nuts.

But there were no raisins or nuts on the breakfast table that morning. There was no cream for his father's coffee either. Just cooked oatmeal, low fat milk, and black coffee.

His mother didn't answer him. She was busy rattling the pans around in the sink. The pans made little raps and clangs. They sounded as if they were jabbing at each other.

"What's the matter?" Pete asked.

His mother only pressed her lips together.

Pete's father came into the kitchen. He closed the door carefully behind him. "Edith is still sleeping," he said, and sat down in his usual place.

There was a piece of adhesive tape stuck on his chin. His father used an old fashioned razor. His father liked a lot of old fashioned things. But cooked oatmeal wasn't one of them.

"Nothing's the matter," answered his mother. Her voice was stretched and airy.

Pete's father heard it, too. He dumped two spoonfuls of sugar into his coffee and sat there stirring it while he gazed at her.

"Nothing at all is the matter," she said again. She came to sit down at the table. This time her voice was even thinner, stretched tighter. Like a pink balloon just before it's going to pop.

Suddenly Pete didn't feel too hungry. He pushed away his bowl of oatmeal.

His father took a gulp of his coffee and set the cup down gently on the table. "Edith is just trying to help," he said. "All she's doing is trying to help."

But his mother wasn't listening to his father. She wasn't talking to his father either. The silence grew. It swelled. It rose above them. It hung over their heads, filling the space over the kitchen table. It grew some more. It filled the whole kitchen.

Pete pushed his chair back. He heard the sound of the chair legs scraping on the floor.

"Ask to be excused!" his father shouted at him before Pete had a chance to say anything.

"Excuse me," his mother said in a small, tight voice. She got up from the table and went up the stairs. Pete heard the bedroom door click as it closed.

Pete stood there for a while.

His father picked up the newspaper and stared at it without reading.

Pete cleared his throat. "I think I'd better go see about something," he said.

His father just kept staring at the same item in the newspaper.

"Excuse me?" said Pete.

His father got up and walked out of the kitchen.

"Where are you going?" Wanda shouted at Pete as he walked slowly, almost reluctantly, down the street.

He shrugged. "Probably over to Miss Patch's house."

She skipped along in front of him, facing him, skipping backwards.

"I was there yesterday," she said.

He stopped. A feeling of dread began to rise in him. Wanda looked happy. She looked entirely too happy.

"So?" he demanded.

"So you weren't," she said.

And for some reason she stepped aside and let him go on down the street by himself. She just stood there and watched him go.

12

MISHMASH MET Pete at the gate. It was just as if the dog had been sitting there waiting for him. Mishmash jumped up and snorted when he saw Pete, he woofed a little. He whinnied, he seemed to thrumm.

Pete got down on his knees and hugged the dog. "I love you, Mish," he whispered. And he was sure, well almost sure, that the dog said the same thing back.

Miss Patch opened the door with a smile on her face. She said, "Come in, Pete." But she didn't say, "Come in, Mishmash." She didn't say anything to Mishmash. She carefully closed the door in front of his face.

"It likes to eat cooked egg white," Miss Patch announced as soon as Pete had come into the house.

Pete looked at the Venus flytrap. Its leaves were fat and glistening.

"It absolutely thrives on hamburger!"

"That's nice," said Pete.

Mishmash's head appeared, framed in the kitchen door window. He was standing on his hind legs looking in. He stood there grinning at Pete.

Miss Patch shook her head at the dog. "He can't resist poking at it," she said. She didn't sound pleased.

Pete went out the front door and came around the house to the back. Mishmash was still standing there, rattling at the doorknob.

"C'mon, Mishmash," Pete said.

Reluctantly, the dog followed. He kept looking back every once in a while. Once he stopped, turned around, and started back.

"MISHMASH!" hollered Pete.

The dog turned and ran beside Pete again.

They walked together past the church with the wooden steeple and down to the gas station on the corner.

Pete put some money into the Coke machine. He flipped the cap off the bottle and took a long, slow drink. Mishmash watched him impatiently.

Pete wiped his mouth with the back of his hand. He offered the dog a drink. The dog grabbed at it and got splattered. He sat back, surprised.

"You have to hold it up to drink from it," Pete said. "You hear me? What you've got to do is tip the bottle up and let the stuff run down your throat."

Pete held it for Mishmash this time, but the dog didn't want any help. He wanted to do it himself. The liquid poured down over his nose. Mishmash yelped.

Pete picked up the empty bottle and set it into the rack.

"Come on, Mishmash," Pete said. "Let's go." They moved down the street.

The rocking chair on Mrs. Berty's front porch was creaking when they passed by. Mrs. Berty's mother was coming around the corner of the house. She waved to them.

She was wearing a carpenter's apron. It had pockets across the front of it. A hammer and a screwdriver were stuck into the pockets.

"I bolted the windows shut," Mrs. Berty's mother said. She untied her apron, rolled it up, and stuck it behind a rose bush. She sat down on the porch with Pete and Mishmash. Then she got up, gave the rocking chair a push, and sat down again.

Pete wondered why she wanted to put bolts in the windows.

"Someone sneaked in and nosed through my stuff," she said in a low voice. She looked back over her shoulder. "Can't find my compass or my emergency blanket."

Pete felt a strange uneasiness creeping up his back. He looked quickly around, too.

"Yesterday I woke up and found my sleeping bag pulled out of my pack. It was dragged every which way on the floor. I didn't tell my daughter, though. She's skittery, if you know what I mean. Just took care of it myself."

She jerked her thumb toward the windows of the house. "Nobody can open them now. Not from the outside, anyway. Don't tell my daughter that."

"I won't," said Pete.

"I'm used to taking care of things. I like to do things for myself. I'd rather walk than ride. I'd rather talk than listen." She nodded at Pete. "I suspect you know that already."

"That's all right," said Pete. "I like to listen."

"I'm used to going places by myself, too. I don't mind hitchhiking. But you've got to be careful. You meet all kinds of people on the road. I used to stop at a gas station and use the facilities. And I'd talk to people who were getting out of their cars to stretch their legs. Got some of my best rides by just talking with people who stopped for gas. Once I slept a hundred miles in the back of a nice truck coming up from California. Real comfortable it was."

Mrs. Berty's mother stopped talking. She bent her head to one side and looked at Mishmash closely.

"You know, I never before saw a dog who looked as if he were really listening."

"Mishmash is a very unusual dog," Pete said and patted the dog's head.

"The way he looks at you—you'd almost think that dog could talk!" said Mrs. Berty's mother. She laughed.

Mishmash looked as if he were laughing, too. His lips parted and his tongue wagged out. And he shook a little, although no sound came from his throat.

"Well, he can't talk!" said Pete positively. That's one thing he didn't have to worry about. Mishmash wouldn't talk.

13

"YOUR AUNT EDITH left," Wanda informed him. She was sitting on his porch steps. "She waited and waited to say goodbye to you," Wanda said, as if it were Pete's fault.

Pete opened his front door and looked in. His mother was in the living room moving all the furniture back where it belonged. He closed the door again.

The sound of Mrs. Barnes' piano floated down the street. It sounded as if she were singing to a lot of hammering. Pete started to walk down the block.

"Where are you going?" shouted Wanda.

Pete didn't bother to answer. She came running up behind him. Pete walked a little faster. The hammering became louder as they got closer to Mrs. Berty's house. A ladder leaned against the wall. A bundle of shingles lay on the ground. Mrs. Berty was standing next to the shingles, looking up.

"You come down from there, Mother! You come down right this minute."

The hammering stopped for a moment. "I will," called Mrs. Berty's mother. "Just as soon as I get this job done." She leaned over the edge of the roof and looked down at them.

Mrs. Berty gasped.

"Do you know this roof has never been shingled properly?" Mrs. Berty's mother said. She made a loud clicking sound with her tongue against her teeth. She shook her head and picked up her hammer again. "I think I might as well shingle the whole roof while I'm about it," she said happily. And she opened a new bag of nails.

"Mother, you can't do that!" Mrs. Berty wailed. And she went inside her house and closed the door.

"She said you can't," Wanda said.

"I heard."

"Can you?"

Mrs. Berty's mother grimaced at them both from the rooftop. "Just watch me."

Wanda sat herself down on the grass and crossed her legs. "She thinks you're too old."

"What she thinks is that old people aren't good for anything anymore," said Mrs. Berty's mother with a sniff. "She thinks they shouldn't do the things everybody else does. Just because they're old." She pounded the hammer down on a nail hard.

"Bake a pie? Can't. Stay up late? Can't. Clean the house? Can't. Climb a tree? Can't. Hitchhike? Can't. Fix a roof? CAN'T!" She began waving her hammer around.

"I've been baking pies and climbing ladders and hitchhiking and fixing roofs all my life. And I don't aim to change now just because I'm older!"

Wanda ducked.

Mrs. Berty's mother put the hammer down. She peered down at them from the top of the house.

"Ever since the first moment I set foot in her house she's been trying to change me."

She pulled some nails out of her carpenter's apron pocket. She stuck a few between her lips, and fitted another shingle into place.

"My mother says she's been trying to change my father since the day they were married," said Wanda.

"What did she want to change him for?" Pete asked.

"She said he could stand a lot of improvement. She said she figured he'd be just about perfect when she got through with him."

"What did your father say?"

Wanda grinned. "He said so far as he was concerned he was just about perfect to start with."

Mrs. Berty's mother turned around and spat some nails out of her mouth. She stuck the handle of the hammer into her armpit and looked down upon them.

"Nobody changes anybody," she said.

Pete wondered if he should tell her how much he had changed Mishmash. Mishmash didn't bark anymore at the plant. And he didn't try to show off by swatting flies. He didn't go in the house on the rug anymore either. Of course, he still poked at the plant. Pete hadn't yet gotten him to stop poking at the plant.

"People have to change themselves," Mrs. Berty's mother said. She dug into the brown paper bag and pulled out another handful of nails. She began to stuff them into the pocket of her carpenter's apron. "And, believe me, changing yourself is the hardest work there is."

She sat there on the roof, pounding down the shingles.

14

"IT'S NICE and peaceful here for a change," Miss Patch said. She plopped down on the sofa and stuck her feet up on the coffee table. She was wearing new shoes. They were flat and wide. Wide enough to wiggle her toes right inside them.

Mishmash must have stopped poking at Wanda's plant, thought Pete. He sat down on the big chair opposite Miss Patch and stretched his feet out, feeling pretty peaceful himself, for a change.

The teacher shoved a plate of cookies toward him. "Take two of them. It's a new recipe. My brother sent it to me. The one called Pete."

Pete took a cooky.

"His zucchini cookies are scrumptious. Almost as good as his rhubarb cake. My brother is a creative cook."

"A what?"

"He never follows a recipe."

"Oh." Pete put the cooky back down on the plate. He shoved the bitten-off part under the rim of another one. "I like things plain and simple," he said.

Miss Patch glanced at him. Her teeth suddenly stuck out. "I know," she said.

"I could take one for Wanda," Pete offered politely.

"Why don't you take one for Mishmash, too."

Pete took one. For Wanda. Mishmash wasn't the kind of dog who liked creative cooking. Not unless he could do it himself.

"Where's Mishmash?" he asked, looking around.

"Oh, somewhere about, I guess," the teacher said.

"Maybe he went to the park," Pete said. "Sometimes he goes there to push at the swings."

Miss Patch was leaning back with her hands clasped behind her neck and her elbows sticking up in the air. Her eyes were closed.

"I think I'll go look for him," said Pete after a little while.

Miss Patch's eyes stayed closed. Her eyelids twitched. Finally her lips moved just a little bit. She said, "If you want to."

"You didn't happen to see Mishmash anywhere around here, did you?" Pete asked Wanda when he reached home.

"If Mishmash were anywhere around here, you'd know it," said Wanda. "Anytime Mishmash is around here, the whole neighborhood knows it."

Pete glared at her.

"If I know Mishmash," Wanda said smugly, "he's probably just lying low. He's probably lying there under Miss Patch's bed or some place, snickering."

"Mishmash doesn't snicker," said Pete.

"Believe me," said Wanda, "if dogs could snicker, that's what Mishmash would be doing."

Pete opened his mouth and closed it again. He certainly wasn't going to argue with Wanda about anything Mishmash could do. As a matter of fact, he wasn't going to argue with Wanda about anything.

15

PETE KNOCKED on the teacher's door. He knocked loudly and shuffled his feet on the doormat. He rang the bell and knocked again.

The door was opened by Wanda. She was wearing a white apron.

"Is Mishmash here?" asked Pete.

"No, he's not," said Wanda. She stood there in a bossy way, not opening the door any further.

"Where's Miss Patch?" Pete asked.

"I'm not sure that she can see you," Wanda announced. "She's very busy."

"I want to tell her I've been looking and looking, and I can't find Mishmash anyplace," Pete said hoarsely.

"Well you can't bother her now with it. Her plant's sick. She's sitting with it right now. She's waiting for the plant doctor to come."

"Didn't you hear me?" Pete demanded. "I said Mishmash is missing."

Miss Patch's face appeared above Wanda's head.

"Oh," she said. "I thought it was the doctor."

"It's me," said Pete. "I can't find Mishmash."

But Miss Patch was looking over his head down the street. A van had stopped down at the next corner.

"Pete," she said, "would you mind running down the street and seeing if that's the plant doctor? Maybe he can't find the house."

Pete walked down the street. He looked into every yard for

Mishmash as he went, just in case. He even looked into the van, parked and headed the other way. It had a metal screen on the back window just like the dog catcher's car. But there were no dogs inside. Only plants.

A man in a rumpled blue shirt was sitting in the driver's seat. He was frowning at something written on the back of an envelope.

"You looking for Miss Patch's house?"

The man looked up. He had white eyebrows and a red beard. He smiled.

"Right," he said. "That's exactly who I'm looking for."

"She lives at the other end of the block. Back there. She's waiting for you."

"You live around here?" the plant doctor called out to him through his open window. He backed up while Pete walked.

"Not far," said Pete, waving his arm in the direction of his house.

"I don't get many calls around this neighborhood. Not house calls that is. Most people who have sick plants bring them to me."

"Did you happen to see a big black dog anywhere around here today?"

"A dog?" he asked, as if he had never heard of one before. "I never pay any attention to dogs. Now if you had asked me whether I had seen a cattail, or a sheep sorrel, or a wild onion, I could tell you right off."

He stopped his car at the curb in front of Miss Patch's house. Pete followed him through the gate up to Miss Patch's front door.

"I'm the plant doctor," the fellow said when Wanda opened the door. He smiled at Wanda.

"I don't carry a black bag when I make house calls," he said. "Just a humidity gauge and a light meter. But I really am a doctor," he told her. "A Ph.D. in botany. I do plant surgery. But I also run a plant store."

He shook hands with Miss Patch.

"I recall one case involving a woman who used peanut shells to drain her plants. I couldn't figure out what was wrong." The doctor rubbed his nose and smiled at Miss Patch. "Until I found out that she was eating salted peanuts and then I knew it was the salt that was killing her plants."

"Miss Patch doesn't eat peanuts," Wanda said.

"If a plant isn't properly taken care of, it is susceptible to pests and disease," he warned. "But, like I always say, a healthy plant can resist almost anything."

He looked around and Miss Patch pointed to the plant sitting in the middle of the kitchen table.

It looked sick, all right, thought Pete. Bloated. As if it had eaten too many flies. A couple of pods had turned black. And some had dropped off.

The doctor lay his humidity gauge and his light meter on the table and squatted on his heels so that his eyes were on a level with the sick looking plant.

"Well, well," he said. "What have we here?"

"It's a Venus flytrap," said Wanda.

"*Dionaea muscipula,*" muttered the plant doctor. "So it is!" He seemed really pleased. "Fascinating!" he said. "I don't see many of these."

Wanda began to swell up with pride. Her chest got bigger and her cheeks fatter.

"There are only about 450 species of carnivores. That means meat-eating plants," the doctor said to Wanda and Pete. "It's hard to believe, but some are capable of devouring lizards and rabbits." The doctor shook his head at the wonder of it. "This one eats flies and insects mostly. I bet there are no flies, ants, or roaches left around this place anymore."

"Not even a gnat," said Miss Patch proudly. Then she added, "Until the day before yesterday, that is."

"Mishmash catches flies," Pete said. But no one heard him.

"What happened the day before yesterday?" the doctor inquired. He put on his glasses and began examining the plant.

"Venus was fine first thing in the morning." Miss Patch sounded worried again. "I left the window open so she could have a good breakfast. I've been doing that lately."

"And?" The doctor seemed absorbed in studying the plant.

Miss Patch raised her shoulders and dropped them again. "Then I went shopping. When I got back, the house was full of flies. But Venus wasn't having any." She looked at the doctor anxiously. "This is the third day it hasn't touched a thing."

"Did Mishmash go shopping with you?" Pete asked.

The doctor motioned for silence. Then he bent his head and put his ear down close to the plant.

Pete heard the buzz of a fly on the ceiling. He heard the drip of the faucet in the bathroom. He heard his stomach rumble.

Miss Patch watched the doctor with an anxious expression. The doctor straightened up. Thoughtfully, he tapped his thumbnail against his front teeth.

He checked his humidity gauge and read his light meter. "Hmm-mm," he said. "Humidity is okay." He looked out the window. "If the sunlight is poor the traps will be smaller and the leaves will be longer," he said absently. He said cheerily, "Well, you've got plenty of sunlight."

"It felt fine," said Miss Patch. "Absolutely fine, until the day before yesterday."

Pete looked out the window. It was the day before yesterday that Mishmash disappeared.

The doctor scratched his red beard. "As far as I can tell—well, I'd say it's probably eaten something that doesn't agree with it."

"The only thing around here that doesn't agree with it—is Mishmash," said Wanda.

Pete stared at her. A shiver whirled up his back. Prickles stirred the top of his head. Fear grabbed at his neck. He saw the meaning of her words coming into Wanda's mind, too. He saw the red fade out of her cheeks and her mouth fell open.

"That's plain ridiculous," Miss Patch said to Wanda. And she laughed.

"Sure it is," said Pete. And he laughed too. He laughed loudly. Only it didn't sound like laughter to his ears. It sounded hollow. Like knocking on a watermelon gone too ripe. Or on a box with nothing in it.

Pete backed away. He went out the door and stumbled down the steps. He ran around the house and banged the front gate behind him.

16

A FLY was buzzing around the garbage can at the gas station. A bee began to make a circle around Pete's head. He ducked to get away from it.

"You see a big black dog anywhere around here?" he asked the man who was fixing a tire. He was a new helper.

"Lots of them," the man said. "Beats me how this neighborhood is running with big black dogs."

"Thanks," said Pete, and he began to move on.

"I'm always chasing them off," the man called after Pete. "I no sooner chase one off than another comes. This morning one of them yanked the gas hose right out of the tank. Boy, that truck driver was mad. Yesterday a big black critter actually got into one of the truck cabs and honked the horn. I never saw anything like it."

"Yesterday!" said Pete. "Did you say yesterday?"

The man wiped his face with a paper towel. "Or maybe it was the day before yesterday."

"Here Mishmash! Here Mishmash! Here Mishmash!" Pete hurriedly went on up the street. He called as loud as he could. As if the sound of his voice could fill the hollow that was getting bigger and bigger inside him. "MISHMASH!" he bellowed into someone's open garage. But the only thing that came out was a poof of dust.

A man stuck his head up from behind a pile of boxes. "My name is Morris," he said crossly.

"You didn't see a big black dog around here today, did you?" Pete asked, even though he already knew that the man hadn't.

"I don't need any dogs," the man said, and he went back to his sweeping.

The mail lady was coming up the street. She nodded at him. "How's everything over at Miss Patch's house?" she asked.

"Her plant's sick," said Pete in a hoarse voice.

The mail lady pulled at some envelopes in the bag hanging from her shoulder. She sorted through a bunch in her hand. "Probably overfeeding," she said. "People are always overwatering and overfeeding their plants. I see it all the time."

"It's a carnivorous plant," Pete said.

The mail lady stopped shuffling the mail. "Personally, I wouldn't have one of those around my house." She shuddered.

"It only eats insects and flies!" Pete bawled after her. But he didn't believe it. He didn't believe it at all.

17

"SOME PEOPLE," said Wanda darkly, "can't see their noses in front of their faces." She threw up her hands. "Talking to them is like talking to a stone wall."

Pete tried not to listen.

"Miss Patch thinks Mishmash ran away. Or got lost. Or something. That's what *she* thinks."

A noise came out of Pete's throat. It sounded like a gargle.

"That's what I said, too," said Wanda. "But *she* said all those stories about carnivorous plants are myths. That they didn't really happen. That they *couldn't* happen."

Pete raised his head. "What stories?"

Wanda closed her eyes. She recited:

"'A recent report is credited to a Brazilian explorer who returned from an expedition that led him into a district of Brazil that borders on Guyana. During this journey he saw a shrub which nourishes itself on animals.'"

She took a deep breath.

"'An explorer and naturalist relates that while botanizing in the swamps of Nicaragua, hunting for specimens, he heard a cry. Running to the spot, he found a monkey caught in a plant. The plant, it is reported, is well known to the natives who tell many stories of its death-dealing powers. Its appetite is voracious and insatiable, and in a few minutes—'"

She interrupted herself—"You want more?"

Pete shook his head.

"Well, I can give you more if you want it. There are plenty more like that in old newspapers in the library."

"You can't believe everything you read in the newspapers," said Pete.

"Who says so?" Wanda sat up straight.

"Your mother."

Wanda looked up at the closed window over their heads.

"Being printed in newspapers isn't proof," said Pete.

Wanda twisted up her mouth. She looked over at him meaningfully. "We *have* proof," she said.

Pete turned his head away. "Maybe it just seems like proof," Pete said. "The fact is—we don't know. We don't really know."

"There are all kinds of books in the library that'll tell you," she said. "They're not all fiction."

Pete felt his Adam's apple slide up and down. Suddenly, he found it hard to swallow.

Wanda's eyes glittered. "There's this book about weird things. It tells how once a year in this certain jungle, a beautiful girl is sacrificed to a horrible tree—"

Pete stood up. "That couldn't happen!" he said.

"Lots of things that people once said couldn't happen are happening," said Wanda calmly. "Like flying into outer space, and walking on the moon, and a woman President."

"I never heard of a woman President," said Pete, feeling suddenly on sure ground.

Wanda smiled to herself. "You will," she said.

Pete went slowly down the street. And he didn't look under any bushes, or behind any garbage cans, or around any more corners.

18

THERE WERE no holes in the teacher's front lawn. No fresh piles. No little brown spots, either. There were no flowers growing upside down in the flower border. No new holes in the hedge. No torn cartons, no bashed in old cereal boxes, no chewed up bones, no pillow dragged out to air.

The shades were neatly pulled on the windows. The welcome mat was in its place in front of the door. Right side up. The front door was open.

"I expect Mishmash will just walk in any day now," Miss Patch said, as if she really believed it. "He never did care to stay away from home for very long."

Pete didn't say anything.

"I washed his old blanket for him and mended his pillow," Miss Patch said.

Pete stood around while Miss Patch spread the blanket on the dog's bed and plumped up the pillow.

Pete watched the teacher put away groceries. "I bought him some People Crackers." She opened the package to show Pete the shapes of a police officer and a mail carrier. "He'll love eating them," she said.

Pete felt a doorknob turning in his throat. He tried to swallow but it wouldn't go all the way down. It was still there the next morning.

"We could put another ad in the newspaper," his mother suggested.

Pete pushed the cereal around in his bowl. "No thank you," he said.

"Or you might try offering a reward and posting it on the supermarket bulletin board," his father said.

"It wouldn't do any good," said Pete.

His mother looked at his father. His father cleared his throat. "Well, why don't we just wait and see," he said lamely. And he picked up the newspaper and held it in front of his face, reading.

His mother picked up the dishes and put them down again. She walked over to the dishwasher and stood there, holding a couple of plates in her hands.

Pete gazed at the other side of the paper. There was a big ad spread over it. PLANT SALE, the headlines said.

Pete turned his head away. He'd have to tell them, he guessed. He wondered how to tell them. Pete picked up his glass of milk. He put the rim to his lips and, without drinking any, set the glass down again. He wasn't hungry. He felt too full of knowing what he knew.

His father turned the paper over. "Hmmmm," he said, looking at the ad. "We need any exotic plants?"

Pete raised his head. Words came out of his mouth, like coffee sloshing out of a cup.

"It doesn't say anything about Venus flytraps, does it?"

His father's eyes appeared over the top of the newspaper, growing rounder and wider. "You aren't thinking of planting any of those around here, are you?"

His mother laughed. It was the first time she had laughed since his Aunt Edith had left.

His father seemed pleased. He rattled the paper and cleared his throat and said, "Of course, if you insist on planting any carnivorous plants in our garden, I suggest you stay away from the front flower border. The one the paper boy jumps over every day. I wouldn't like missing my morning paper."

His mother laughed again.

Pete stood up. "Stop it! Why don't you just stop it!"

They gaped at him. His mother blinked with surprise. His father forgot to hold the newspaper up. The lower corner dipped into his coffee cup.

"You don't know anything about anything!" Pete shouted at them. And he ran out, slamming the door.

19

"I THOUGHT you'd come out sooner or later," Wanda said. She was sitting on her front porch. She had her mother's old black sweater around her shoulders. There was a black hairbow half falling out of her hair. A box of tissues lay on the step beside her.

Pete sat down, too. "They don't know yet." Pete had a hard time getting the words out of his throat and past his teeth. There didn't seem to be any space inside there anymore.

Wanda stuck her arms through the sleeves of her mother's black sweater. "Miss Patch doesn't know yet either," she said. "No one knows yet. No one but you and me."

Pete glanced at her and began to feel a little uneasy. Wanda looked almost as if she were pleased.

She caught his glance and sighed, heavily. "Ten days have gone by," she said in a meaningful low voice.

Ten days. Pete remembered. The doctor had said it took ten days for the Venus flytrap to digest its food. Pete tried not to think of what the doctor said. He told himself he wasn't going to think about it.

"My mother and father still want to put ads in the newspapers," he said. "They are still talking about putting notices up on the lost-and-found board at the supermarket."

Wanda pulled a tissue from the box at her side and swabbed her eyes. "Miss Patch is still leaving the door open every night in case he comes back. She doesn't know he's never coming back."

The words hung out in the air before them. They were as clear as letters cut from ice. They wouldn't go away. *He's never coming back.*

Wanda blew her nose. "It's my fault," she said. Pete didn't disagree with her.

Wanda stopped wiping her nose. She sat there all slumped over as if she were feeling sorry for herself. "You think it's my fault, don't you?"

Pete didn't intend to answer. He looked across the lawn to the street. He saw Mrs. Berty's little red car go by. He saw a big truck turning at the end of the street. Across the way, Mrs. Anderson was just going back into her house with a sack of groceries in each arm. She was having trouble opening the screen door. She flicked it with her elbow, and held it open with her behind as she fumbled in her purse for the key.

He thought of Mishmash poking at doorbells and looking into windows. He thought of Mishmash wanting to help hang clothes and carry groceries and deliver packages. He thought of how much he hated Wanda Sparling.

"I said," said Wanda, poking at him, "you think it's my fault, don't you? Don't you!"

"Leave me alone," he said. He jumped up and faced her with his hands clenched. "JUST LEAVE ME ALONE. If you don't leave me alone, I'll—"

Wanda stood up, her hands on her hips, her chin stuck out. "You'll what?"

Pete pulled his head back, and his elbows, too. His arm shot out. His fist punched Wanda in the stomach.

"Owwwwwwwwwwuuu!" hollered Wanda. She jumped on him. It seemed to Pete as if the whole world had landed on his chest.

They rolled over and over, across the front lawn and down to the sidewalk. There was a roaring in Pete's head. Like a ten-ton truck. A screeching in his ears. Like the sound of tires. A horn was honking.

Or was that Wanda snorting in his face?

Then someone else jumped on him. Someone big and black and hairy, with a slathering wet tongue.

Mishmash.

20

"HE'S BACK!" Pete heard himself hollering. "Mishmash is back!"

Mishmash began to bark. He stepped all over Pete. He thumped his tail on Pete's head and slapped a wet tongue over Wanda's face.

"FEEEEEAUGHHH!" screeched Wanda. She covered her face with her hands and hastily got up.

A truck was parked at the curb. Its red sides were pink with dust. Rain had splattered it. The painted yellow letters on the side said WESTERN VAN LINES. And underneath that was WE HAUL ANYWHERE.

The cab door swung open. The driver jumped out. She wore Levi's and a pink ruffled blouse. Her hair was short and curly. She seemed pretty glad to see them.

"He was hitchhiking," she said.

"HITCHHIKING!" hollered Wanda. Her face was redder than a tomato.

"Well, that's what he was doing so far as I could make out. He was standing with some kids where the road turns into the freeway. And when they jumped in, he jumped in, too."

Pete held onto Mishmash and grinned.

"It wasn't until the kids got off that I discovered the dog was on his own." She scratched her nose. "Never before have I met up with a hitchhiking dog," she said.

"There never was a dog like Mishmash," Pete said. "You should see what he can do!"

The woman backed away hastily. "No thank you," she said. She hopped into the cab of her truck and locked both doors.

Mishmash stood there watching the truck move off, and then he started off, too—toward the teacher's house.

Pete followed him.

"Wait for me!" shouted Wanda, and she came running after them.

The dog began to trot as he reached the end of the block. His trot broke into a run a little further on. And by the time he reached the gas station, he was leaping along far ahead of them.

They heard yipping and yapping and pounding and barking before they even got to the gate. It sounded as if Mishmash was standing on the welcome mat hammering on the door.

Pete and Wanda came through the front gate just as Miss Patch opened the door. She began yapping and yipping herself when she saw the dog. She hugged and squeezed and patted him. And she had to take out her handkerchief and blow her nose and wipe off her glasses.

Mishmash sat on the welcome mat panting, his mouth grinning open, and his tongue hanging out. He walked into the house and looked around.

Wanda's plant was no longer there in the middle of the kitchen table, Pete noticed. It was sitting in the living room window between an African violet and a potato plant. Along with all the other plants. Mishmash came out and sat down again on the welcome mat.

"He must have hitchhiked both ways," said Pete, feeling proud.

Mishmash blinked his eyes. He yawned. A fly buzzed around his ears. He rolled his eyes and twitched but he didn't bother to do anything about it.

Miss Patch patted him some more. "I guess he's a little wiser now," she said happily.

"My mother says that travelling is very educational," said Wanda.

"She says you can learn a lot just getting out of your own neighborhood. She says—"

"I wonder if Mishmash learned to drink Coca Cola out of a bottle," said Pete. "He never knew how to drink it from the bottle before."

Wanda snorted.

"He's probably a little thirsty right now," said Miss Patch. "He's probably hungry, too." And she went into the house.

"How's Venus?" Wanda loudly called after the teacher. But Miss Patch was too busy opening and shutting cupboard doors to hear her.

Mishmash stood up. He turned himself around a few times and flopped down. He rested his head on his forepaws and closed his eyes.

"He'll probably sleep for a week," said Wanda, as if she would be glad if he did.

"So will Miss Patch," Pete said. And he couldn't help adding, "Now that she doesn't have to worry about Mishmash."

Wanda glared at him. "You think everybody around here is always so worried about Mishmash," she said. "That's all you ever think about is *Mishmash*. Mishmash in the morning. Mishmash at noon. Mishmash every night." Wanda's voice was growing louder and louder.

Mrs. Tribble, who lived next door, opened her front door and looked out.

"It's Mishmash *here*," shouted Wanda. "And Mishmash *there*. It's Mishmash everywhere you go!" Wanda stuck her neck out so that her face was pushing into Pete's. "You know what I think?"

Pete pulled his head back quickly. He never knew what Wanda was thinking.

"I think your whole world is one big MISHMASH! That's what I think!"

And Wanda went down the walk and out the gate and up the street.

Pete watched her go. For once, he felt a little sorry for Wanda. It was plain to see that her Venus flytrap plant was no longer the teacher's pet.

Next door, Mrs. Tribble came out on her porch. "My petunias are coming up real nice this summer," she called over to Pete. "Right side up."

Pete looked over the fence at the neat border of petunias. He glanced back at Miss Patch's porch where Mishmash was sleeping soundly. Only Mishmash wasn't exactly asleep. One eye was open. It was looking in the direction of Mrs. Tribble's petunias. And on one side of the dog's face a grin was beginning to show.

Pete looked at the flowers, then back at the dog. He shook his head and frowned hard at Mishmash.

The dog stopped grinning. He closed his eye. Then he opened it again.

Pete sighed. He went out the gate and carefully latched it behind him. *Nobody changes anybody*, he thought as he turned toward home. His mother couldn't change his Aunt Edith. Mrs. Berty couldn't change her mother. And no matter how hard anyone tried, no one could change Mishmash.

Pete took a deep breath. That was a relief to know. Not until this moment did he realize what an immense relief it was.